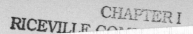

# Wh~~~~

Missy's cheeks ~~~~~~. "I'm not leaving this house until you give me back my tape!"

"What tape?" said Stephanie.

Missy folded her arms. Too late to turn back now. "The one you stole! The video tape about my family for the school project!"

Stephanie's eyes grew wide. "I did not!" she said.

Missy glanced around the room. She had never felt so discouraged in her life. With a loud sigh, she grabbed her coat, wrapped it around her waist, and let herself out the door. "I know you have it somewhere, Stephanie," she called over her shoulder, "and I'm going to find it!"

# VIDEO STARS

by Molly Albright

illustrated by Eulala Conner

**Troll Associates**

*Library of Congress Cataloging-in-Publication Data*

Albright, Molly.
     Video stars / by Molly Albright; illustrated by Eulala Conner.
          p.     cm.
     Summary: Disaster stalks Missy's attempts to make the best
video tape of self and family for a class assignment until her
actress-grandmother comes to the rescue.
     ISBN 0-8167-1480-0 (lib. bdg.)          ISBN 0-8167-1481-9 (pbk.)
     [1. Schools—Fiction.   2. Family life—Fiction.]   I. Conner,
Eulala, ill.   II. Title.
PZ7.A325Vi   1989
[Fic]—dc19                                                     88-15880

The publisher gratefully acknowledges the use of lyrics:

OH WHAT A BEAUTIFUL MORNING by Richard Rodgers & Oscar Hammerstein II
Copyright © 1943 by Richard Rodgers & Oscar Hammerstein II
Copyright Renewed
All Rights Administered by CHAPPELL & CO., INC. International
Copyright Secured
ALL RIGHTS RESERVED

A TROLL BOOK, published by Troll Associates,
Mahwah, NJ 07430

# VIDEO STARS

# CHAPTER

# 1

——————

It was a rainy, cloudy Thursday morning. Missy Fremont hurried into her classroom at Hills Point School and shook out her umbrella. She could hear her friend Wilhelmina Wagnalls calling to her from the hall.

"Missy, wait up," Willie shouted.

When Missy turned around, she burst out laughing.

"What's so funny?" said Willie.

"Where'd you get that raincoat?" Missy giggled. "It looks like it belongs to your father."

"It does." Willie grinned. She flapped her arms and turned around. "Isn't it neat?"

Missy nodded.

"How come you weren't on the bus today?" Willie asked.

"Mom and I had to drop Baby off at the pet groomer's," Missy said. "He's getting a flea bath and haircut." Baby was Missy's Old English sheepdog and her best friend.

Missy's neighbor and classmate, Stephanie Cook, walked over. "Baby has *fleas*?" she said, butting into the conversation. She shuddered and took one step back. "I hope they don't spread through the neighborhood."

Missy frowned. Ever since she and Baby had moved to Indianapolis from Cincinnati last fall, Stephanie had been giving them both a hard time. Missy's nickname for Stephanie was Ms. Perfect.

"Don't worry, Stephanie," Willie interrupted in a good-natured voice. She pretended to pick something off Missy's head. "So far only Missy and her dad have them."

Missy shook her head and grinned. Wilhelmina loved to kid around with people.

"That's disgusting," said Stephanie, wrinkling her nose. She stared at Willie's raincoat. "What's *that* supposed to be?"

Missy and Willie quickly exchanged glances. "Can't you tell?" said Missy with a straight face. "It's Willie's new designer raincoat."

Willie nodded solemnly. "It cost a fortune. I got it a few sizes too big so I could grow into it."

Stephanie leaned over to inspect the raincoat. "Seriously?"

Willie puffed up her cheeks to keep from laughing. "Seriously." Two seconds later she exploded.

Stephanie's eyes narrowed. "Ha, ha. Very funny. Don't you think I know a smelly old hand-me-down when I see one?"

"It's not a hand-me-down!" Willie said indignantly. "My dad still wears this!"

Before Stephanie had a chance to reply, the first bell rang. Everyone hurried inside. Missy's teacher, Ms. Van Sickel, was already writing something on the board. "Take your seats, class," she said. "We've got lots to discuss today."

Missy quickly slid into her chair and tried to see what Ms. Van Sickel was writing. It was time to start another class project and Missy was anxious to find out what it was.

Missy saw the words ANCESTORS and INTERESTS printed on the board. What could Ms. Van Sickel mean?

"Class," said Ms. Van Sickel, "remember when we were learning about the different types of advertising and we wrote and recorded our own TV commercials?"

Missy nodded her head enthusiastically. She and Emily Green had done one for pizza-flavored toothpaste. Emily had played the mother and Missy was a little girl who hated to brush. Ms. Van Sickel thought the commercials were so spectacular that she got Mr. Lewis, the school principal, to show them at a special schoolwide assembly.

"I know how much everyone enjoyed working with the video camera," Ms. Van Sickel continued, "so I've come up with another project where we can use the camera again." Ms. Van Sickel took a deep breath. "I thought it would be interesting if each student was given an opportunity to use the camera for one week to make a movie about his or her family."

"Wow! That's neat!" said David Holt. "You mean we get to take the camera home with us?"

Ms. Van Sickel nodded. "I think you're all responsible enough to take care of the camera, don't you?"

"Definitely!" said Ashley Woods and Amy Flanders together.

"But what are we supposed to talk about?" asked Lawrence Shoemaker.

Ms. Van Sickel smiled and turned to the blackboard. "I was wondering when you'd get to that. You can introduce us to your family. Show us any special interest you have, any family hobbies. You might even want to talk about your ancestors, where they came from, what they did for a living. I'm going to leave it up to you. The only requirement is that you make it no longer than thirty minutes."

"That's easy," said Adam Ramirez.

"Not as easy as you'd think." Ms. Van Sickel smiled. "It might make good sense to sit down and figure out exactly what you want to do before you start." She held up a piece of paper. "I'm going to pass around a sign-up sheet for the camera."

"Ms. Van Sickel," said Stephanie. "My father just bought a brand-new camcorder. Can I use that instead?"

Missy rolled her eyes. Ms. Perfect was already trying to figure out a way to look better than everyone else.

"I suppose so," Ms. Van Sickel said.

Stephanie folded her arms and glanced around the room with a smug expression.

"Any more questions?" said Ms. Van Sickel.

The class was quiet. "Good. I look forward to seeing your projects."

Later during lunch everyone was talking about the project again. "I can't wait," Amy was saying. "I'm going to get Winston to do his imitation of George Washington crossing the Delaware." Amy's brother Winston was very funny. He wanted to be either a comedian or an astronaut when he grew up.

A girl who Missy didn't know too well spoke up next. Her name was Isabel Mendoza. "My cousin Teresa lives in Spain," she said in her quiet voice. "I can talk about her. She lives in a small fishing village in Galicia."

"Where's that?" Willie asked.

"It's above Portugal," Isabel explained. "Teresa and I are the same age. We're pen pals."

"That's really neat," said Emily. "I wish I had an exciting family."

"*My* ancestors came from England," said Stephanie. "There was even a duke in the family."

"Are you sure he wasn't a *cook*?" said Missy, making a joke about Stephanie's last name.

Everyone except Stephanie laughed. "Where's *your* family from, Missy?" she asked. "I'll bet you don't even know."

"Stephanie!" said Emily. "That's not a very nice thing to say!" Missy had been adopted by the Fremonts when she was a tiny baby.

Missy realized that everybody was staring at her. "Baby and I are two of a kind. We came from outer space," she said solemnly. "Our mother was an asteroid and our father was a Martian." To her relief, everyone laughed again.

The lunch bell rang. "Time for music appreciation," said Amy.

As Missy walked down the hall, she started thinking about what Stephanie had said to her. What *was* she going to talk about? She had no idea where her real parents came from.

"Boo!" said Willie behind her.

Missy jumped about a foot.

"What were you thinking about?" asked Willie.

"Nothing," said Missy.

"You looked like you were in outer space," said Willie.

"I was," Missy grinned. "I was talking to some asteroids."

Willie stuck her fingers on top of her head as if they were antennae and wiggled them back and forth. "Beep, beep. This is your uncle Proton. Why haven't you written? Beep, beep." She spun around and headed back toward the cafeteria.

Missy playfully tugged on Willie's arm. "This way, Uncle Proton," she said. "You don't want to miss music appreciation, do you?"

"Beep, beep. No way," said Willie. She aimed her antennae toward the classroom door and shuffled inside. "Are you coming, earthling?"

"I'm right behind you," Missy giggled.

# CHAPTER

# 2

———

"**M**om, where did I come from?" Missy asked. She and her mother were sitting at the kitchen table after school having a little snack.

"You came from an adoption agency," she said. "Is that what you mean?"

"Not exactly," Missy answered. She explained about the class project and how some people were going to talk about their ancestors.

Missy's mother listened carefully and then nodded. "I see your point," she said. "But I don't really know the answer." She reached over and gave Missy a big hug. "I've never thought of you as anything other than a Fremont."

"Neither have I," Missy admitted.

"Besides," her mother added, "the Fremont family is quite colorful. How many kids do you know that have a father who plays viola with the Indianapolis Symphony?"

"Or a mother who teaches kindergarten and gives piano lessons," said Missy.

"Or a dog who thinks he's a person," said her mother with a smile. Baby, who had been napping peacefully under the table, perked up his ears.

Mrs. Fremont pulled a brochure out of the stack of mail that had arrived that day. "Speaking of doing interesting things," she said, "I've just signed up for a gourmet cooking class." She leafed through the brochure until she found the right page. "See?" She pointed. "We'll be cooking a different recipe each week. This week it's pork chops in prune sauce."

Missy wrinkled her nose and Baby whimpered.

"You haven't even tried them yet," her mother said.

"We don't need to," said Missy.

Missy heard the front door shut and watched her father walk into the kitchen. "And how are the beautiful Fremont women this afternoon?" he said, putting his viola case down on the table.

Missy's mother blushed.

"How was your rehearsal, Dad?" asked Missy. Mr. Fremont rehearsed with the symphony every day until about 3:30. Twice a year he got to go on tour to some exciting city like New York or Boston. He always brought back good souvenirs for Missy and Baby.

"Not bad, not bad." He felt inside his coat pocket. "Now, what did I do with my keys?"

"Maybe you left them in the front door," said Missy. Her father was forever misplacing things.

Mr. Fremont nodded and headed back to the hall. "Here they are," he called.

Missy and her mother looked at each other and grinned.

When Mr. Fremont returned to the kitchen, Missy told him about the class project. "School sure has changed since we were kids," he said.

"Right," said Missy. "I'll bet you had to walk two miles every day through the freezing snow."

"I'm not *that* old," laughed her father. "That's a story my mom used to tell *me*."

Missy tried to picture her grandma Fremont bundled up and trudging through the snow. "I miss Grandma," she said suddenly. "When's she coming to visit?" Missy's grandmother still lived in Cincinnati. She was sort of roly-poly looking and drove a '58 turquoise Cadillac convertible called "Alice."

"Dad has a solo in two weeks," said Mrs. Fremont. "Last time we spoke she said she was going to try to come if she didn't have rehearsals." Missy's grandmother had a very good voice, and she frequently appeared at the Red Barn Dinner Theater. Missy had seen her play Miss Hannigan in *Annie*.

Baby wandered out from underneath the kitchen table, shook himself all over, and then sneezed.

"Bless you," said Missy, her father, and her mother all at once.

"Baby got a haircut today," said Missy to her father.

"I noticed," he said. "Smells like he had a flea bath, too." Now Missy's father sneezed. "Achoo!"

"Bless you," said Missy and her mother for the second time.

"Maybe you should take Baby to the park to air him out a little," said Mrs. Fremont. "That flea dip is pretty strong."

Missy nodded. "Good idea, Mom. Let's go, Baby." Baby tucked his tail between his legs and followed Missy out the front door.

"*Arf, arf!*" he barked, wagging his tail.

"Settle down," said Missy.

Baby leapt up and then rolled onto the lawn, waving his paws in the air.

"Baby! No!" said Missy. "You just had a bath."

Baby rolled some more and then shook himself.

"You're going to get dirty," warned Missy, pulling him up by the collar and heading toward the sidewalk.

Baby obediently followed Missy down the street. At the end of the block was the little park where Missy and Baby liked to walk. Usually no one was there and Missy sometimes liked to pretend that it belonged to them.

Baby ran through the gates and immediately rolled in the grass again.

"Will you stop it?" said Missy. "What's the point of having a bath?"

Baby reluctantly stood and shook himself off.

"Let's go to the playground," said Missy. At the other end of the park was a Jungle gym, a few rusty swings, and a slide.

Missy no sooner sat down on the bottom of

the slide when Baby began to roll again, this time in the sand. "Baby Fremont!" she yelled. "What did I tell you? No rolling!" Missy raised her hand to give Baby a swat on his behind.

"*Arf,*" yelped Baby, dodging out of the way. He took off across the playground.

"Come back," shouted Missy.

Baby disappeared around the corner.

Reluctantly, Missy stood up. "Baby, come here," she called. "I'm sorry I tried to spank you."

Baby didn't answer.

With a sigh, Missy started after him. "Where are you? I said I was sorry. What more do you want?"

Beside the water fountain were two old green benches. Underneath one of them a pair of familiar brown eyes stared out at her. "Aha!" she said.

When Baby saw Missy he shrank farther under the bench. "Oh, stop. You're being silly." Missy suddenly froze. "Uh-oh." On top of the bench was a large sign. WET PAINT, it said.

"Come on out, Baby," she coaxed. "I'm not mad. I promise. Just don't get any paint on yourself."

Slowly, Baby wiggled out. First his head and then his belly. "Too late." Missy sighed. Two long green stripes ran from his head down to his tail.

Baby shoved his wet nose into Missy's hand.

"It's okay," she said glumly. "It's not your fault you can't read."

"Missy!" shrieked a familiar voice. "What happened to Baby?"

Missy looked up and saw Stephanie standing beside the drinking fountain, balancing back and forth on her roller skates. Just her luck! "Hi, Stephanie," she mumbled. "Baby got some paint on himself."

"Paint doesn't come off," said Stephanie. "He's going to look like a green skunk for the rest of his life." To prove her point, she pulled a clean handkerchief out of her shoulder purse and blotted it on Baby's fur.

Missy pinched her lips together. "Are you sure?"

"Positive," said Stephanie, waving the hankie in Missy's face. "Look. It already dried on him."

Missy sneezed. "What's that smell?"

"Mustique," said Stephanie, shoving the scented hankie back under Missy's nose. "Don't you love it?"

Baby flattened his ears and growled. He hated perfume.

Stephanie took a small spray bottle out of her purse and squirted a dose behind her ears. "Want some?"

Baby growled a second time. "No, thanks," Missy said quickly.

Stephanie daintily put the bottle back in her bag and set her purse on the edge of the fountain. She leaned forward to study Baby's fur. "A dog has to be pretty stupid to get into paint."

"He's not stupid!" Missy bristled. "Sheepdogs

happen to be one of the most intelligent dog breeds in the world."

"Ha!" said Stephanie.

Missy took several stiff steps forward. "Excuse us, please."

"Where are you going?"

"To our house," said Missy. "I'm sure once I give Baby a bath this paint will come right out."

As Stephanie reluctantly stepped aside, Baby suddenly reached behind her. "Hey!" said Stephanie. "What do you think you're doing?"

Baby grabbed Stephanie's purse and took off.

"Come back here, you thief," cried Stephanie.

Baby bent his head down and galloped to the far side of the park. "Baby, no!" said Missy. She watched in amazement as Baby stopped and began to dig furiously.

"Oh my gosh," screamed Stephanie. "He's going to bury it!"

"Bad dog," said Missy, trying to sound strict.

"Missy, you have to stop him!" said Stephanie. "I can't go on the grass with my skates on."

"Baby, come here!" said Missy, this time a little firmer. She'd never known Baby to bury anything. It must be the perfume.

Baby wagged his tail and kept digging.

"Missy!" said Stephanie. "That's a brand-new bottle of Mustique in there and *you're* going to have to pay for it."

Baby wagged his tail and dropped the purse into the hole.

"Okay, okay," said Missy. She reluctantly crossed the park and retrieved the purse just as

Baby was about to cover it completely. "Cut it out, Baby," she whispered. "You're getting me into trouble."

She returned the purse to Stephanie. "Here."

Stephanie carefully brushed the dirt off. "Ruined," she muttered. "I told you your dog was stupid."

"No stupider than your perfume," Missy shot back.

"Humph!" said Stephanie.

Missy grabbed Baby's collar. "Come on, Baby," she said. "Let's go home and give you a bath."

Later that evening Missy stood watching Baby shivering in the bathtub. She'd been scrubbing for nearly two hours. "It's just no use," she sighed.

Missy's father stuck his head inside the door. "Any luck?"

"Baby's going to be green for the rest of his life," Missy said in a tearful voice. She pointed to a scrub pad and a pile of rags. "I've tried everything."

Baby flattened his ears and whined.

"Now, now," said Mr. Fremont, patting Missy's arm. "It'll wear off eventually."

Missy sniffled. "Are you sure?"

"Of course. In another month or so Baby will be back to his normal self."

Missy stared woefully at Baby. "I sure hope you're right, Dad."

The next morning as Missy made her way across the street to the bus stop she could see

Stephanie standing holding a clipboard. Several of the little kids were clustered around her.

"Stephanie's hiring people to be in her movie," one of the little girls announced. "I get to play one of Stephanie's friends when Stephanie was in kindergarten."

Missy wrinkled her nose. Stephanie reeked of Mustique.

"It was my first dance recital," Stephanie announced to everyone at the bus stop. She gave the little girl a pat on the head. "You're going to get to wear a costume and everything."

"Hooray!" said the little girl. She clapped her hands together and skipped in a circle. "Costumes!"

"Aren't you getting a little carried away?" said Missy.

"No," said Stephanie. "I'm doing a musical about my life. *The Stephanie Cook Story*."

Missy raised her eyebrows but didn't say anything. She couldn't believe that anyone would take Stephanie seriously.

By recess Stephanie had signed up most of the girls in their class. "I promise everyone will have costumes," she kept saying. "And a friend of my father's is going to write some original music."

Missy tried to keep from throwing up.

"Can we wear makeup?" asked Ashley.

"Of course," said Stephanie. "I might even get a makeup artist." Several of the girls squealed with delight.

"Are you going to be in Stephanie's movie?" Missy whispered into Willie's ear.

Willie shook her head. "I don't look good in a tutu."

Stephanie put her hands on her hips. "It's not polite to whisper in front of other people. And anyway, I heard what you said."

"No, you didn't," said Willie.

Stephanie glared at the two of them. "I suppose your videos are going to be better?"

"Much better," Missy shot back. She glanced wildly around the room. "In my video, Baby's going to do some spectacular tricks."

Willie looked at her with surprise.

"I've already begun training him," she continued boldly. "He's going to jump through a hoop while catching a Frisbee."

"Humph," said Stephanie. "A green dog who does tricks. Big deal. What's that have to do with your family?"

"Baby is a part of our family," Missy said. She raised her voice slightly. "You won't believe how good *my* video is going to turn out. I can't wait."

"Me neither," said Willie under her breath.

Missy pretended not to hear. Green dog or not, she was determined to produce the best video of all.

# CHAPTER

# 3

The next morning Missy stood in her back yard with Baby. In one hand she held an old hula hoop and in the other a hard-boiled egg. Hard-boiled eggs were Baby's favorite snack. "Baby, jump!" she shouted, waving the egg in front of Baby's nose.

Baby wagged his tail and trotted around the hula hoop.

"That's not what I meant," said Missy. She took a few steps back. "Try again."

This time Baby ducked under the hula hoop and grabbed the egg out of Missy's hand. "No!" she said. Before Missy could catch him, Baby ran to the other side of the yard and dug a hole to bury the egg.

Missy sighed. Ever since Baby had buried Stephanie's purse, he'd been burying everything in sight. "Baby," she said patiently, "we've been out here for almost an hour now. When are you going to catch on?" She glanced around the yard and noticed one of Mrs. Fremont's piano students leaving their house. "Hey, Jimmy," she called. "Could you help me? I need someone to hold this hoop."

Jimmy Keegan was a few years younger than Missy. She didn't really know him, but she'd seen him around school.

"Okay," said Jimmy. He put down his sheet music and ran over. "What happened to Baby?"

"He got into some paint." Missy handed Jimmy the hula hoop. "Here. Are you strong enough to hold this?"

Jimmy braced his legs and lifted the hoop. "Easy."

Missy stood behind Baby. "Jump," she said. She bent down and tried to lift Baby off the ground. It felt like he weighed a ton. "Aaargh," she grunted.

Baby's rear end slowly lifted off the ground. He walked forward on his two front paws and crashed into the hoop.

"Are you trying to do a wheelbarrow race?" asked Jimmy.

Missy shook her head. She sat Baby's rear end back down. "Watch." Missy got down on all fours and barked. "Jimmy," she hissed. "Say 'Jump, Baby.'"

"Jump, Baby."

Missy hopped through the hoop. Jimmy started laughing.

"What's so funny?"

"Nothing."

"Then why are you laughing?"

Jimmy shrugged.

Missy hopped through the hoop a few more times. "Now you try it, Baby."

Baby looked at Missy and wagged his tail. "Jump, Baby," she said. Baby sat down.

"I don't think he understands you," said Jimmy. He squirmed from one foot to the other. "My arm is getting tired."

"Never mind, then," said Missy. "This isn't working anyway." She took Baby back inside the house and went upstairs to use the phone.

"Hello, Willie?" Missy said. "I need some help." She was lying down on the rug at the foot of her bed. The phone cord stretched from her parents' bedroom under the door and into her room.

"What is it?" said Willie.

"I'm having a problem teaching Baby his trick. I thought if maybe someone helped me, it would make it a little easier."

"I thought that's what you were going to say," said Willie. Missy could hear Willie's brother yelling something in the background. "Just a minute," Willie said. The phone crashed to the floor. "If you pull on me one more time, I'm not going to let you be in my movie," she heard Willie scream. "Now, where were we?" Willie continued politely.

"Baby," said Missy.

"You want me to come over tomorrow afternoon?"

"That would be great," said Missy.

The next afternoon Willie, Missy, and Baby

were sitting in the back yard. Beside them was a bowl of hard-boiled eggs.

"Here's my suggestion," Willie was saying. "I'll hold the hoop on the ground and you lead Baby through. Each time he does it right he gets a bite of hard-boiled egg. After he gets the idea, we'll raise the hoop a little more and a little more until *bam*! He's jumping through the hoop."

"It sounds tiring," said Missy, thinking about all the jumping she was going to have to do. "But worth it," she added quickly. "What about teaching him the Frisbee part?"

"Later," said Willie. "He's already a good catcher."

By five o'clock Baby was already hopping about three inches. "Do you think Baby needs a rest?" puffed Missy.

"Maybe we should stop for the day," said Willie.

"I'll trade places with you if you want," said Missy.

Willie squinted her eyes. "No, thanks. I don't think I'll fit through the hoop."

"Willie! Missy!" called someone from the front yard. "Anybody home?"

Missy saw Ashley walk around the corner.

"What are you doing here?" said Willie.

"I have a costume fitting at Stephanie's," she replied. She looked at Baby and sneezed.

"Want me to put him inside?" asked Missy. Ashley was allergic to dogs.

Ashley shook her head. "I just wanted to see how his trick was coming."

"It's coming along pretty well," said Missy.

"We're actually teaching him several tricks. It's very complicated."

Ashley nodded and stared at Baby's back. "What happened to his fur?"

"It's part of his costume," said Missy. "Do you like it?"

"I guess," said Ashley. She sneezed again. "You should see the costumes Stephanie is ordering for us. Pink and gold with sequins. We're all going to march down this staircase singing and walk onto this special stage that Mr. Cook ordered from New York. It's going to be beautiful."

"Sounds like it," said Willie.

"Well, I guess I'd better go," said Ashley.

Missy and Willie quietly watched Ashley walk away. "Gosh," said Missy finally. All of a sudden, Baby's spectacular tricks didn't seem so spectacular after all.

"Dad," said Missy at dinner. "Remember that lemonade stand you built for me once?"

A couple of months before, Missy's father had built the stand to help Missy raise money for a class trip. She and Stephanie had been competing like mad to see who could raise the most cash. And it hadn't helped that Missy's stand had been the most rickety thing she'd ever seen.

Just remembering that project made Mrs. Fremont laugh.

"Pat!" said Missy's father. "There was nothing wrong with that lemonade stand."

"I was wondering if you could build me and Baby a little stage," Missy continued, ignoring her parents.

"Baby and me," said Mrs. Fremont.

Missy gave her mother an exasperated look. "Mom! Do you mind? I'm trying to talk to Dad about something."

"You're right, honey," said her mother. "I'm sorry I interrupted."

Missy noticed her father shove most of his pork chop in prune sauce underneath a large lettuce leaf. "I want to teach Baby a few tricks to perform for my video," she explained.

"I think I could manage a small stage," said Mr. Fremont.

"Good," said Missy. She turned to her mother. "What about you?"

"What about me?" said her mother, teasing.

"Do you think you could make Baby a costume? Something that would cover up his stripes?"

Now Missy's father started laughing.

"Cut it out, you guys," said Missy.

Mrs. Fremont leaned over and kissed Missy on top of her head. "I'd be happy to sew Baby a costume," she said, looking right at Missy's father. "On one condition."

"What's that?" said Missy.

Mrs. Fremont smiled. "I want you to at least try your pork chops."

"But, Mom!" Missy slouched down in her chair. "Okay," she said reluctantly. "One bite."

"Three," said her mother.

"Three," muttered Missy. She leaned under the table and stared at Baby. "I hope you're appreciating this."

Baby thumped his tail against the floor and barked happily.

# CHAPTER

# 4

"**M**om, do you think you could make this?" said Missy. She pointed to a picture she'd found in a library book of a dog in a circus costume.

Mrs. Fremont stared at the photograph and frowned. It had been about a week since Missy's parents had promised to help her and Missy was starting to get anxious.

"I'm not sure I could duplicate the hat," Mrs. Fremont said finally.

"What about the ruffles?"

Mrs. Fremont sighed. "Ruffles are tricky. Besides, Baby might have a hard time fitting through the hoop with all that on."

Missy tried not to look too disappointed.

"Want to know what I had in mind?" said her mother brightly. "We'll take one of Dad's old T-shirts, dye it a pretty color, and decorate it!"

Missy wrinkled her nose. "Ugh."

"I think it would be adorable," her mother persisted. "We could even make you a matching one."

Missy thought about Stephanie's pink and gold sequins. "You sure it wouldn't look stupid?"

"Absolutely not," said her mother. "Come on, I'll show you."

Several hours later Mrs. Fremont held up two freshly dyed bright pink T-shirts. "What do you think?"

"Not bad," said Missy.

"They'll be darling once we decorate them," said her mother. She dug through one of her knickknack boxes. "These feathers might look cute."

Mr. Fremont stuck his head inside the door and stared at his T-shirts. "I hope you don't expect me to wear those."

Missy laughed. "How was your performance, Dad?" Her father was still dressed in his tuxedo.

"That darned Charlie Butler beat me in poker again," he said. During intermission a lot of the musicians played cards.

"Do you like our costumes?" said Missy. "We still have to decorate them."

"What happened to the ruffles?"

"We thought this would be cuter, William," interrupted Mrs. Fremont.

"What about the stage?" said Missy quickly. "I get the camera next week."

"Hmm," said her father. "How about Saturday?"

"It's a deal," said Missy.

*　*　*

Missy couldn't wait for Saturday. That week she and Willie perfected Baby's trick. Even the costumes turned out pretty well. Missy trimmed the sleeves with gold braid and glued rhinestones down the backs. Everything was going to work out perfectly.

Saturday morning Missy and her father began early. "Now, what did you have in mind?" said her father, waving a cup of coffee.

"Could you make it a platform with a wall on the back?" said Missy.

"Don't see why not. We'll need a couple of sheets of plywood and some two by fours."

"We can use the wood from my lemonade stand," said Missy. "Want me to draw up a plan?"

"Nah," said her father. "Piece of cake."

Because the saw was so rusty, it took most of the morning to cut the wood. It also took a while to find the hammer, which Baby had carried off to bury in the back yard. "I'm supposed to go over to Willie's soon," said Missy. "I promised to help her with the last part of her video."

"You go ahead." Mr. Fremont waved. "I can nail this thing together by myself."

"Are you sure?" said Missy. Her father had a habit of missing the nails.

"Go on, honey," he said. "It'll be done when you get home."

Twenty minutes later Missy and Baby arrived at Willie's house. "Finally," said Willie, opening the door. Missy could see Willie's little brother,

David, racing up and down the stairs. "I told him he could be in the movie today and he's been acting hyper ever since," Willie explained.

Missy nodded. She noticed Willie had combed her hair and was wearing some eyeshadow and lip gloss. "What do you want us to do?"

"I'm going to give a tour of our tree house," Willie said. "I want you to be the cameraperson."

Missy nodded. She and Baby followed Willie and David to the back yard.

The Wagnalls had the best tree house Missy had ever seen. It was even better than the tree house in *Swiss Family Robinson*.

Willie and David scrambled up the ladder to the first platform. Beneath them on the lowest branch an old tire dangled from a rope. "Should I start shooting?" said Missy. She braced her legs and positioned the camera on her shoulder.

Willie nodded. "Go ahead and start." She smiled broadly. "This is our tree house," she began. "It's been here for almost twenty years. Every family that has lived in this house has added something to it."

Missy turned and did a shot of the Wagnalls' house for dramatic effect.

"We call this first platform The Living Room," Willie continued. David started waving his arms and gesturing at the platform. "Stop it, David," said Willie, pulling him down onto the old couch that they had somehow managed to drag up there. David punched his sister in the arm.

"This is where I come to get away from my

brother," said Willie, glaring at David. "Sometimes I even sleep up here."

"Only once," David interrupted. "And it wasn't because you had permission. You were running away from home."

Willie's face turned red. "Do you mind?" she said. David slouched back on to the couch and folded his arms.

"The second platform is called The Lookout," Willie continued.

"For obvious reasons," added David.

Willie grabbed David's arm and twisted it. "But right now it's where I'd like to throw my brother David off."

"Ow! That hurts," he said. "I'm telling."

Down on the ground Baby whined impatiently and nudged Missy's leg. "Stop it, Baby," Missy whispered. "You're jiggling the camera. Go sit on the other side of the tire." Baby slunk away.

Up on the platform Willie had purposely shifted her position now so that David was completely blocked. "The first improvement we made," she was saying, "was adding the sofa." Two fingers appeared behind Willie's head and wiggled back and forth. Willie knocked the hand down. "Next," said Willie, standing up, "David added this little shelf so we wouldn't have to bother Mom all the time for glasses."

David's head popped around from behind Willie's back. "That's me," he said, waving.

With one big shove, Willie pushed David back onto the couch. "Next time you interrupt you're leaving!" she thundered.

David crossed his legs and muttered something to himself.

"Now, where were we?" said Willie politely.

"Hey, look what I just found!" David said, completely ignoring his sister. "My Frisbee!"

"I'm warning you, David," said Willie.

David waved the Frisbee in the air. Down on the ground Baby's ears perked up. "Here, Baby!" he said. "Catch!"

Willie grabbed the Frisbee from David's hands. "Let go, you little creep," she said.

"Make me," said David. With one powerful tug, he wrestled the Frisbee away from his sister and sailed it off the platform.

Missy couldn't believe what happened next. As the camera continued to whir away, Baby leapt up and shot through the rubber tire just as they'd practiced. "Baby, no!" she yelled. Before Baby's feet landed back on the ground, his jaws snapped neatly around the Frisbee.

"Wow! Good catch!" said David.

"Cut, cut," yelled Willie. She put her arm around David's neck. "I'm going to strangle you," she said. "That was Baby's trick that we've been practicing for days now."

David waved his arms weakly in the air. "Mom, help."

Willie let go. "You worm," she said with disgust. She scrambled down the ladder.

On the ground Baby was wagging his tail proudly. "Baby!" said Missy. "You're supposed to do that trick for *my* video, not Willie's." Baby

barked and then hopped through the tire several more times.

Willie shook her fist at her brother. "You're going to get it now," she said.

"How was I supposed to know?" he answered.

"All our hard work," Missy moaned.

"Maybe you can teach him another trick," said Willie.

"But it's my turn to have the camera on Monday," said Missy. "He'll never learn another trick by then."

"Then he can do this one again," said Willie, glaring up at David. "Anyway, it'll look completely different when he's in costume on the stage."

Missy looked doubtful.

"Don't worry, Missy," said Willie. "No one will even know it's the same trick."

"Are you sure?"

"Positive. Wait till you see how nice it'll look on the stage."

Missy looked up at David, who was busy examining his bruises, and sighed.

"You're lucky you're an only child," said Willie, reading her thoughts. "Little brothers are a pain."

Missy's father was waiting for her outside the garage when she got home. Missy hoped Willie was right about the stage. "Finished?" she asked.

"Yep." Her father grinned. "Take a look." He threw open the garage door.

Missy's heart sank. It wasn't at all what she had in mind. "It's nice, Dad," she said. She didn't want to hurt her father's feelings, especially after he'd worked so hard. "Do you think it's too small?"

"Nah. Try it out," said her father.

Missy ran to get her hoop and stood on the tiny platform. "Okay, Baby. Jump."

Baby leapt through the hoop and landed on the far side of the garage, missing the stage by four feet.

"Maybe you should move farther left," said her father.

Missy stood on the very edge. "Try again, Baby," she said.

This time Baby went flying through the hoop and landed in the middle of the stage, crashing through the plywood.

"Baby! Are you okay?" said Missy.

Baby struggled out of the hole and wagged his tail.

"I was afraid that might happen," said Mr. Fremont.

Missy stared at the hole Baby had made. "Can you fix it?"

"Maybe," said Mr. Fremont.

Baby whined and leaned against the back wall.

"Watch out!" Mr. Fremont shouted again. The back wall slammed to the floor.

"Dad!" wailed Missy. "It's falling apart."

"Now, let's not panic," said her father. "I'm sure it can be repaired. I just didn't brace it properly." He picked up his hammer and started to nail another board onto the back. "Ow!" Mr.

Fremont grabbed his thumb and started hopping up and down in a little circle.

"Did you hit yourself?" said Missy.

"Ow, ow, ow," said Mr. Fremont. He held out his hand for Missy to see. His thumb was already starting to puff up. "Good thing I don't have another performance until Wednesday," he said weakly.

Missy looked out the garage door. Ashley, Amy, and Emily were walking past. "Hi, Missy," Emily called. "What are you doing?"

"Building my stage," said Missy.

Emily held up a dress bag. "We got our costumes. Want to see?"

Before Missy had a chance to say no, Emily unzipped the bag and took out a beautiful pink-and-gold sequined outfit. "Aren't they wonderful?" she shouted.

Missy nodded glumly and then turned around and stared sadly at her stage. "I'm going inside for a bandage," said her father. "Sorry about this, honey."

Missy sat quietly for a few minutes. Her stage was ruined, her costumes looked like they were made by a first grader, and Baby had already performed his trick for Willie's video. "Well, Baby," she said finally. "Now what?"

# CHAPTER

# 5

*B*eep, beep, beep.

Missy was still sitting on the garage floor. She looked out to see who was honking.

An old turquoise Cadillac pulled into the driveway and honked again.

"Grandma!" shouted Missy. She raced over to the car and threw open the door.

"Golly. You've grown six inches!" said her grandmother as she tumbled out and gave Missy a big hug. Baby waddled over and wagged his tail.

"I forgot you were coming," said Missy, giving her grandmother another hug. "Boy, am I glad to see you."

Grandma's eyes twinkled. "Forgot your old granny already, huh?"

"No way!" said Missy. She took Grandma's hand and pulled her toward the house. "Mom! Dad! Look who's here!"

"Mom!" said Mr. Fremont, hurrying out the garage door. "Glad you could make it."

"You know I've never missed any of your solos yet," she said smiling. "I'm more dependable than the postman."

Mr. Fremont laughed and gave her a kiss. "That's for sure."

Grandma stared at Mr. Fremont's hand. "What happened to your thumb, Billy?" No one called Missy's father "Billy" except for Grandma.

"Nothing. I just banged it with a hammer."

Missy's grandmother shook her head and clucked like a chicken. She noticed the stage. "Oh, my. Look at that! Planning a show of your own, Billy?"

"I'm supposed to be making a movie about our family for a class project," said Missy. "Baby and I were going to do an act on it." She stared sadly at the hole.

Grandma didn't seem to notice. "How about that!" she said proudly. "She's pure Fremont, isn't she, Billy?"

"Verna! How was your trip?" said Missy's mother, coming out of the house. Missy didn't know anyone else named Verna. Sometimes she suspected her grandmother had made it up.

"Hello, Pat," said her grandmother. "Good to see you." She and Missy's mother hugged.

"William, why don't you help your mother with her suitcase?" said Mrs. Fremont. "I'm sure she's ready to come inside and put her feet up." She opened Alice's back door and two shopping bags full of soda cans, an old blanket, and a tissue box tumbled out.

"One of these days I'm going to have to clean the car," said Grandma.

"Mom, where's your suitcase?" laughed Missy's father.

"Everything's in that cardboard box. I couldn't find my suitcase when I was packing."

Missy's father shook his head and grinned.

"You're just in time for dinner," said Mrs. Fremont, smiling. "Why don't we all go inside and have some supper and you can unpack later?"

"I'll help," said Missy. She couldn't wait to see what her grandmother had in that cardboard box. It was filled to the top.

"I've got a surprise in there for you," said her grandmother, reading her mind. Her eyes sparkled.

"What is it?" said Missy.

"Later, later," her grandmother sang. "Come on, little munchkin. Time for supper."

After dinner Missy and Baby hurried to the guest room to be with Grandma. She'd already spilled most of the cardboard box onto her bed and was trying to fold everything into neat piles. "I'm not much of a packer," she said, pulling a pair of slippers with feathers on the toes out of the box.

Baby sniffed the slippers and sneezed.

"Bless you," said Grandma. She peered into the box once more. "Oops. Almost forgot your surprise. Close your eyes."

Missy felt her grandmother put something heavy and beaded on her lap.

"Open."

Missy stared down and gasped. "It's beautiful. What is it?"

"A flapper dress. It belonged to my mother back in the Roaring Twenties."

Missy held the dress up. It was covered with shiny purple, gold, and green beads that formed a pattern down the back and front. "Don't you want it?"

"I'm too fat," laughed Grandma. "Besides, I thought you'd like to have something that had been in the family for a long time. Try it on. I'm sure it'll fit."

Missy slid the dress over her clothes. It had a low waist, a V neckline, and short sleeves. She turned slowly in front of the mirror. "I love it!"

"Fits like a glove." Grandma nodded. "Can you Charleston?"

"What's that?"

"A dance people did in the twenties. Watch." Grandma began humming a tune and kicking up her heels.

When it was over, Missy applauded wildly and Baby barked. "Bravo! Bravo! Encore!" yelled Missy, just as people did at the symphony.

Grandma took a bow. "My mother loved that dance," she said. "Did you know she performed on Broadway?"

Missy shook her head.

"She could have had a great career," Grandma continued, "but then she met my father. In those days, women didn't combine marriage and careers."

"Was she pretty?" said Missy.

"Very," Grandma replied. "Curly red hair, just like yours. She wore it piled on top of her head." She tilted her chin and looked at Missy. "I think I might still have some pictures of her out in the trunk. Want to see?"

"Sure!" said Missy. She and Baby eagerly followed Grandma down the stairs.

When they reached the driveway, Grandma started fumbling around in her pockets. "Now, what did I do with my keys?"

"Are they in the ignition?" said Missy with a grin.

Grandma looked at the dashboard. "How'd you know?"

Missy laughed. "Practice."

Grandma opened up the trunk. "Keep your eyes peeled for some photo albums," she said, digging through the mess. "There should be three of them in here somewhere."

Missy spotted something under the spare tire. "Is that them?"

"Good work," said Grandma. She carefully pulled out the cracked and peeling books. "Presenting the Fremont family!" she said as she opened the top one.

Missy stared at the first page. An old yellowed photograph showed a young boy about Missy's age dressed in knee-length pants and a bow tie.

"That's your great-great-grandfather John Milton Wallace," she said. "He was named after John Milton, the poet. They did things like that back then. He had a brother named Prince Albert."

Missy giggled.

"John Milton came to this country all by himself in 1900, when he was twelve years old. He got a job as a tailor."

"Did he ever see his mom and dad again?" said Missy.

Grandma shook her head. "That was a long way in those days."

"Do you think he was lonely?" Missy asked.

"Yes, I imagine he was. But Prince Albert came to live with him a few years later. The two brothers ended up marrying two sisters!"

"Was one of them the owner of this dress?" said Missy.

"No. That was John Milton's daughter, Emma. Emma is my mother and your great-grandmother." Missy tried to put all these ancestors in order.

"Look. Here's Emma." Grandma pointed. "Wasn't she beautiful?"

In the photograph Emma stood beside a large chair, her hands resting delicately on the back. Her dress looked similar to the one Missy had on, only not as fancy. "This must have been her party dress," Missy said, looking down.

"I expect so," nodded Grandma.

From the street a voice called, "Missy? Is that you?"

Missy strained her eyes. It was almost dark. "Who is it?"

Ashley ran up the driveway. "Is that your costume for your video?" she gasped. "It's gorgeous!"

Missy looked down at Emma's dress. "Uh, yes,"

she said slowly. "Yes, it is!" Grandma winked at her.

"Does Baby have a matching one?" said Ashley.

Missy glanced at her grandmother. "Uh, no. This was my great-grandmother's dress. She danced the Charleston in it. On Broadway!"

"Are *you* going to dance the Charleston?" said Ashley. She was obviously impressed.

Missy's grandmother gave her a tiny nod. "Uh, yes!" said Missy. "Yes, I am!" She gestured toward her grandmother. "This is my grandma Verna. She's an actress in Cincinnati. She played Miss Hannigan in *Annie*."

"Wow," said Ashley. "I never met an actress before."

"There are lots of interesting people in our family," Missy continued. "Want to see some pictures?" She showed Ashley the photos of John Milton and Emma.

"Your video is going to be really neat," Ashley sighed. "Your whole family is talented." A horn honked. "That's probably my mom," she said. "She thinks I'm at Stephanie's. Bye." She disappeared into the darkness.

Missy smiled at her grandmother. "Do you really think I can learn the Charleston?"

"Anybody can Charleston," said Grandma. "Especially a Fremont."

Missy gave her grandmother a big hug. "Thanks, Grandma," she said. "You may not know it, but you just saved my life!"

# CHAPTER

# 6

---

The next evening Missy stood in the living room with the video camera perched uneasily on her shoulder. "Action!" she yelled.

In front of her, Grandma Fremont sat in a rocking chair, the photo albums balanced on her lap. "This is the story of the Fremont family," she began. "Move in closer, Missy honey."

Missy aimed the camera at the photograph of John Milton. "The earliest relative that I know about was this fella, John Milton Wallace," said Grandma. "He was named after the poet." Grandma went on to tell how John Milton came to this country. She even threw in some things Missy hadn't heard before, like how John Milton always carried a lucky penny and how he ate oatmeal and sausage every day for breakfast.

Missy waited until Grandma gave her the secret signal to shut off the camera. Before they'd started shooting, they'd agreed that when Grandma folded her hands, that meant to cut. Missy had gotten the idea from her father, because whenever she went to see him play in the symphony, he would scratch behind his ear to signal that he saw her.

"Now what?" said Missy, after she put the camera down.

"Now we practice the Charleston," said Grandma. Missy's grandmother had the whole thing organized. While Missy danced, Mr. and Mrs. Fremont were going to play the viola and piano and Grandma was going to sing. They weren't going to use the stage at all. Grandma convinced Missy's father that it was too small and rickety to hold the entire family.

"Grandma," said Missy as she moved the coffee table and chair out of the way, "I wish Baby could do something."

"I thought he was still going to try his trick."

Missy shook her head. "I changed my mind." She reached over and scratched Baby behind the ears. "Look! The paint is fading away. You hardly even notice it anymore."

"What'd I tell you?" said Grandma. She clapped her hands. "On stage, everyone. Last rehearsal before the big event." They were going to shoot this part as soon as Missy's father got home.

Grandma tapped her foot on the floor. "And a one and a two . . ." She began to sing the words to the Charleston.

Missy chewed her bottom lip and tried to concentrate. It was hard getting her arms and legs coordinated at the same time.

"Smile, honey," Grandma yelled in between verses. "Looks good!"

Missy grinned at her grandmother. The more she danced, the smoother it started to feel.

"Now the knees," her grandmother shouted.

This was Missy's favorite part. You were supposed to crouch down and flap your knees together while you crossed your hands in front of them.

"Perfect!" said the grandmother.

Missy finished the dance without making a single mistake.

"Don't forget to bow!" said Grandma.

Missy curtsied gracefully.

"Fantastic!" said her grandmother, giving her a big hug. "If I didn't know better, I'd think it were Emma herself."

Missy smiled. "Now is it time to change into our costumes?"

Grandma looked at her watch. "Billy should be home any minute." Mr. Fremont had promised to wear his symphony tux for the video.

Missy grabbed Baby's collar. "Come on, Baby," she said. "Help me get dressed."

On the way upstairs Missy knocked on the door to her parents' room. "Mom," she called. "It's almost time to do our act. Are you ready?"

Mrs. Fremont opened the door. "How do I look?" She was dressed in a calf-length skirt with a long overblouse. She'd combed her short hair forward and added little spit curls to it, just as women did in the twenties.

"Wow! You look like a real flapper person."

"I made these hats for us," said Mrs. Fremont. She handed Missy a ribbon headband with feathers and rhinestones glued onto the front. "I thought since you weren't wearing the other costumes . . ."

"These are terrific, Mom!" said Missy.

"I even made one for Baby," said her mother. She knelt down and wrapped it around Baby's head. "What do you think?"

Baby wagged his tail. "Perfect." Missy laughed.

It only took a few minutes for Missy to change into her costume. She ran down the hall to the guest room. "I'm ready, Grandma," she called through the door. Grandma had promised to help her with her makeup after she was dressed.

"Come on in," said Grandma. Missy's grandmother was bent over the cardboard box. She was wearing her red and orange Japanese kimono bathrobe. "I thought I brought my granny dress," she said. "Do you see it anywhere?"

Missy looked around the room. There were clothes everywhere. Missy had once overheard her father tell her mother that Grandma didn't believe in using drawers. "Maybe you left your dress in Alice," said Missy. "Want me to go check?"

Grandma had managed to squeeze her top half under the bed. "Never mind," she cried. "Here it is. Aarrgh." She pulled herself back out.

"Can you do my makeup now?" Missy asked.

Grandma stared at Missy's head. "Where'd you get that cute hat?"

"Mom made one for each of us. Even Baby."

"Nice," said Grandma.

It took forever for everyone to get ready. Missy had arranged the camera on a tripod, so that everyone could be in the movie together.

"Grandma, put Baby between you and Mom," Missy directed. "Sit, Baby." When Baby was sitting, you couldn't see the green paint at all.

Missy's father tuned his viola. He looked handsome in his tuxedo. "Okay, honey. Let's get this show on the road."

Missy started the camera and signaled to Grandma. "Back in the 1920s," Grandma said, "there was a period called the Roaring Twenties. It was a wild time. The First World War was over, and people felt like celebrating. Missy's great-grandmother, Emma Wallace, was one of those gals." She signaled toward the piano. "Hit it, you two."

Mr. and Mrs. Fremont started playing the music for the Charleston.

As Grandma sang, Missy danced her way in front of the camera. Her hands and feet moved to the rhythm. "Smile, honey," she heard Grandma whisper.

Just then a loud yowl came from behind the piano. Missy looked down. Baby had lifted his chin and was singing along with the music. "*Aaooow, aaooow, aaooow,*" he howled. The feathers on Baby's hat shook as he sang.

Missy grinned and moved aside slightly so that everyone could see him. When it came time for the part where just Missy's parents were sup-

posed to play, Baby continued to sing along. His voice blended perfectly.

After the song was over, Missy ran to turn the camera off. "That was so good! Can we watch it on the TV now?"

Mrs. Fremont put the tape into the VCR. Everyone sat and watched it three times. "I think you've got a winner here," said Mr. Fremont.

"Yeah!" said Missy. "Especially Baby." She leaned down and gave him a kiss. "You didn't tell me you were practicing a trick on your own, did you?"

Baby wagged his tail and barked.

Missy turned to her grandmother. "Grandma, why don't you move here? You could stay in the guest room."

Grandma laughed. "What about the Little Theater? What about my friends?"

"You could make new friends, just like I did. And there are lots of theaters in Indianapolis. Right, Dad?"

Mr. Fremont cleared his throat. "Right."

Grandma bent down and wrapped her arms around Missy. "Honey, that's a wonderful invitation and you can be sure that it's tempting, but I'm happy where I am. Besides, rehearsals for *Oklahoma!* start in two days."

"But Baby and I don't want you to leave," said Missy.

Grandma gave Missy a squeeze. "Maybe if your mom and dad give you permission, you two can come stay with me for a few days and see the show!"

Missy looked expectantly at her parents.

"I don't see why not," said her mother.

"Yippee," said Missy. She took the tape out of the VCR and sat it on the top of the piano. She couldn't wait until it was her turn to show it to the class.

Grandma left early the next day. She said she wanted to get a head start on the traffic. Missy had gotten up with her and tried to help her pack, but even so, Grandma left about five things behind.

"Don't worry," Missy's mother told her. "I'll mail everything back tomorrow."

All day, Missy talked about how exciting her tape was going to be. During recess Stephanie came up to her and said, "I hear you're wearing a costume for your video. I hope you're not planning to copy me."

Missy just shrugged. She wasn't going to let Stephanie get to her this time.

"What does your costume look like?" Stephanie persisted.

Missy smiled. "You'll see," she said. "All I can tell you is that my grandmother brought me a dress that's been in the Fremont family for many years."

"Humph," said Stephanie. "A hand-me-down."

Missy's eyes narrowed. "You're just jealous," she said and walked away.

When Missy got home, she could hear her mother giving a piano lesson to someone in the living room. Missy sat down at the kitchen table and made herself a snack of potato chips, cheezies, and grape soda.

Baby nuzzled her hand.

"Just one," she said, slipping a potato chip under the table to him. Baby took the potato chip and disappeared into the living room. She heard her mother tell her piano student good-by. "Mom," she said as her mother walked into the kitchen, "can we watch my tape again?"

"I don't see why not," she answered. "I don't have any more students today."

Missy ran to the living room. She didn't see the tape anywhere. "Mom, what did you do with it?" she called.

"Nothing. It's on the piano."

"No, it's not," said Missy. She checked inside the VCR, on the sofa. She even looked inside the piano bench. "I don't see it," she said finally. "You must have moved it."

Mrs. Fremont came back. "I didn't touch it," she said. "It's got to be here somewhere."

Missy looked some more. She searched under the TV, under the piano, inside the stereo cabinet. She started to get worried.

Mrs. Fremont looked puzzled. "I don't understand how it could have vanished," she said.

Missy's head felt like it was spinning. How could her tape be missing?

"Why don't I call your father at the symphony hall?" she said. Missy heard her mother dial the number. A few minutes later she returned. "He said he didn't touch it."

Missy's eyes filled with tears. "Mom," she wailed, "what are we going to do?"

Missy's mother patted her arm. "Now, now. I'm sure it's here somewhere. We just have to keep looking."

Just then Baby trotted into the room. "Baby, my tape is missing," Missy said tearfully. She flopped down miserably on the sofa.

Baby looked at her with his big brown eyes and slowly wagged his tail back and forth. His paws were covered with dirt again.

Missy absent-mindedly scratched Baby behind his ears. "*Now* what have you buried," she said in an irritated voice.

Baby's tail thumped back and forth. Tiny particles of mud fell off his whiskers and onto the sofa.

Suddenly Missy sat up and gasped.

"What is it?" said her mother. "What's wrong?"

Speechlessly, Missy pointed at Baby's paws and then stared out the window. "Mom, I just had a terrible thought. Do you think . . . ?"

Her mother's eyes opened wide. "He wouldn't dare!" she said.

Missy jumped off the couch. "Oh, yes, he would," she said, dashing out the back door. "I'll bet you anything Baby's gone and buried my tape in the yard!"

# CHAPTER

# 7

"**B**aby Fremont, you get out here right now." Missy stood in the middle of the back yard, her hands on her hips. Surrounding her were dozens of freshly dug holes.

Baby slunk out the door.

"I've never seen this many holes in my life!" Missy said. "How am I supposed to find the tape in all this mess?"

Baby lay down and stuck his nose between his paws.

With an exasperated sigh Missy knelt to the ground and started digging in one of the holes. "I can't believe you did this," she muttered, scooping the dirt out with her hands. "Who knows where my tape is? It could be anywhere in the yard." Her fingers hit something hard. "Aha!" She dug some more and then pried the object loose. "My autograph book!" she exclaimed. "What's *that* doing in here?"

Baby stared at the ground.

"Never mind," she said, glaring. "I won't ask." She crawled on all fours to the next hole. Inside were two chewed-up pencils and a half-eaten plum.

"Baby, this is disgusting," said Missy, tossing the plum over her shoulder. "What's gotten into you?"

Baby stared at her remorsefully.

Missy surveyed the lawn. It looked like it had been attacked by moles. "Wait till Dad and Mom see this," she said. "They are *not* going to be pleased." She pulled a package of carrots and a box of paper clips out of the next hole. "Where did you bury the tape? Do you even remember?"

Baby peered around the yard like he was trying to concentrate.

"Was it over there?" Missy said. "Think."

Baby shook his head and barked.

"Show me where," said Missy. "*Please,* Baby. This is very important."

Baby ran to the other side of the lawn and stopped beside an apple tree.

Missy hurried over. "Are you sure?"

Baby sniffed at the hole and barked some more.

Kneeling down, Missy started scraping away the dirt. "Good dog," she kept saying. "I'm very proud of you for pointing it out."

She felt something hard again and gave a tug. "Oh yuck!" She threw the remnants of a half-eaten pork chop in prune sauce down on the ground and pointed an accusing finger at Baby. "You don't know where you buried it, do you? You forgot."

Baby hung his head.

"Honey, did you find it?" called her mother out the door.

"Not yet," said Missy, trying to sound hopeful.

"Why don't you get the shovel out of the garage?" called her mother. "It might make it easier to look."

"A steam shovel would be more like it," Missy grumbled.

She decided to try another approach. "Baby," she said in her nicest voice, "I worked really long and hard on that tape. If I don't find it, I'm going to be very, very unhappy."

Baby pawed aimlessly at the ground. Then he looked at Missy and whimpered.

"I give up," she said, heading for the garage. "I guess I'll just have to dig up the whole yard until I find it."

One hour later Missy was still digging when Stephanie strolled into the yard. "Planning a trip to China?" she asked.

Missy wiped a bead of sweat off her nose. "Very funny." Beside her was a pile of things she'd recovered. These included a comb, some violin rosin, four matching coasters, two wooden spoons, and an old Barbie doll.

Stephanie stared at the pile with interest. "I don't suppose you'd tell me what you're doing," she said.

"Not in a million years," Missy answered.

From inside the house, Missy's mother called, "Honey, did you find your tape yet?"

Missy's face turned red.

"I thought so!" Stephanie crowed. "Baby buried your tape, didn't he?"

Missy protectively grabbed Baby's collar. "So what if he did?"

"Serves you right!" Stephanie said. "Now you know how it feels!"

Missy's skin bristled. "He didn't do it on purpose," she said.

"I guess we won't be showing our tapes together next Monday," Stephanie continued. She skipped away cheerfully. "Too bad."

Missy threw down her shovel in disgust and stomped into the house.

"Any luck?" said her mother.

"None," said Missy. "I dug up every hole in the yard."

Missy's mother got down on her hands and knees and looked underneath the piano again. "Then maybe he didn't bury it," she said. "Maybe it's here somewhere." She felt underneath the pedals. "It couldn't have just disappeared. I saw it right before Denise started her lesson."

Missy suddenly stopped. Everything was starting to make sense. "Denise *Cook* was here this afternoon? *Stephanie's* little sister?" Missy gasped. "Mom, why didn't you *tell* me?"

"You know Denise has a lesson every Monday afternoon," said her mother. "What's so strange about that?" She reached up and felt along the piano's edge.

"Mom!" wailed Missy. "You let Denise Cook near my tape!"

Mrs. Fremont sat forward and bumped her head

on the bottom of the piano. "Ow," she said. She looked at Missy. "What are you talking about?"

"I'll bet you anything Stephanie told her to steal my tape," Missy answered. "Then she blamed it on Baby."

"That's ridiculous," said Mrs. Fremont, rubbing her head. "How would Stephanie know that your tape would just happen to be sitting on our piano?"

Missy wasn't listening. "Stephanie told her to be on the lookout. She saw her chance and took it." Missy stared at her mother. "Did you see Denise leave?" she asked.

"She let herself out." Mrs. Fremont sighed. "Missy, I don't like the way you're thinking. You're going on very shady evidence here."

"But, Mom," Missy said. "Stephanie will do anything to be the best. That's how she is."

Mrs. Fremont crawled back out. "Don't you think you're jumping to conclusions?"

"No," said Missy stubbornly. "Not when it comes to Stephanie."

"Let's wait another day or two and see if it turns up," said her mother.

"What if it doesn't?"

"Then I guess we'll have to make another one," said her mother.

"But Grandma's not here," said Missy. "And I already gave the camera to Ashley."

"Missy, let's try not to worry so much," said her mother. "I'm sure we're going to find it."

Mrs. Fremont was bent over a cookbook in the kitchen when Missy got home from school the next day. "Hi, sweetie," she said. "How was your day?"

"Terrible," Missy replied. "I couldn't stop thinking about the tape, I was the last person chosen for dodge ball in gym, and we had creamed spinach for lunch." She sat down with a thud. "Did you find the tape?"

Mrs. Fremont shook her head.

"I knew it," said Missy. "Where's Baby?"

He trotted in from the living room.

"Did he bury anything else?"

"I caught him sneaking off with a bag of grass seed," said her mother. "I think he's trying to make up for the damage." She pointed to the cookbook. "I'm fixing cheese and spinach crepes for dinner tonight. Doesn't that sound delicious?"

"I guess," said Missy. She stared off into space.

Mrs. Fremont sat down beside her. "Why don't we try to make another tape?" she said gently.

"It won't be the same without Grandma," said Missy. "Or the photo albums."

"Dad and I can sing while you dance. It'll look fine."

"Mom," said Missy. "Dad can't play the viola and sing at the same time."

"So then Baby and I will sing," said her mother. "And you can tell the story of John Milton."

Missy nodded reluctantly. Her mother handed her the phone.

"Here. Call Ashley and see when you can borrow the camera."

"Okay," said Missy. "But I don't think this is going to work out."

\*　　\*　　\*

The next afternoon Missy stood outside Ashley's house and rang the bell. Ashley had promised she could use the camera after she was finished.

Missy waited several minutes and then rang again. "What took you so long?" she said when Ashley finally answered the door.

Ashley's face was all red and puffy. "I knew I shouldn't have eaten that tuna fish for lunch," she said. She motioned for Missy to come in.

Ashley's mother came running over. "Hello, Missy," she said. She turned to Ashley with a worried expression. "You shouldn't be walking around, pumpkin."

Missy stared at Ashley's bloated face. She really did look like a pumpkin. "How long are you going to stay puffy?" she asked.

"Probably until tomorrow," Ashley said. "I'm allergic to fish oil." She turned weakly toward her mother. "Could you help me up the stairs, Mommy?"

"What about the camera?" said Missy.

"I haven't used it yet," Ashley replied. She wrapped her arm around her mother's waist. "Maybe tomorrow."

Ashley wasn't in school the next day or the next. When Missy showed up unannounced at Ashley's house on Thursday, Ashley looked completely normal. "How are you feeling?" Missy asked.

"Okay," said Ashley. She rubbed her face. "My skin got stretched out. I have to put a special salve on it."

Missy nodded politely. "Did you have a chance to use the camera yet?"

"No," said Ashley. "I had to go to the doctor's this morning and then this afternoon I napped." She sighed loudly. "If I'm not feeling too weak, I'll try to use it tonight, okay?"

"Okay," said Missy. She tried not to panic. How was she ever going to finish the tape by Monday?

Missy finally got the camera the next day, Friday. Mr. Fremont had a performance that evening, so as soon as Missy got home, she rushed around the living room, trying to set everything up. Her plan was to try to finish the part with both her parents before her father had to leave at 6:30.

"What's going on?" said her mother, when she got home.

"Hurry, Mom," said Missy. "Ashley finally finished with the camera. We're going to do the Charleston part as soon as Dad gets home."

Mrs. Fremont took off her jacket and looked around the living room. "But I have two pupils coming. And you and Dad were going to work on the lawn, remember?"

Missy groaned. "I forgot. Maybe Dad and I can do the lawn tomorrow. What time will you be finished?"

"Five-thirty." The doorbell rang and Mrs. Fremont looked at her watch. "That should be Tommy now."

While Mrs. Fremont gave her piano lessons, Missy changed into her costume. She tried to do her makeup herself but it didn't come out very well. She couldn't get the lipstick to go on evenly.

When Missy heard her father come home, she hurried downstairs to meet him. "Dad, is it okay if we do the lawn tomorrow? I want to do the tape over now and you have to change into your tux."

Mr. Fremont hadn't even put down his viola yet. "Uh, sure," he said. He stared at Missy's face. "Hey, have you been wrestling with Baby again?"

Missy glanced in the hall mirror. "Does my lipstick look too crooked?" she said, wiping her mouth with the back of her hand.

"No, sweetie, it's fine." He grinned.

Finally everyone was dressed and ready to go. Missy arranged her parents and Baby exactly as they had been for the first tape. Missy said her little speech and motioned to her parents to begin.

Mrs. Fremont started to sing the Charleston. Missy had never realized how thin her mother's voice sounded.

"Louder, Mom," hissed Missy. She noticed that her mother's hat had slipped over one eye.

Mrs. Fremont cranked up the volume, but her voice started cracking. Baby looked at Mrs. Fremont and started to growl.

"Baby, *no*!" whispered Missy.

Missy's mother sang bravely on. "Whee," she said, twirling her pinkie in the air. Missy grimaced.

Onstage, Baby's hair stood up on his back. The louder Mrs. Fremont sang, the louder he growled. "Whee!" she said again, trying to cover Baby's growls.

It was time for Missy to dance onstage. As she

crossed the room, she deliberately stopped in front of Baby, blocking him from the camera.

Baby growled even louder and tried to get around her. Missy pushed him back with one arm as she continued to dance with the other.

Out of the corner of her eye Missy could see her father edging over toward Baby. When he got close enough, he tried to use his leg to try and shove Baby behind the sofa. Baby didn't budge.

Missy was so busy worrying about everything that she lost her place. She tried to make something up but it was too late. The song was finished. Missy took a clumsy bow and hurried over to shut off the camera. "That was terrible!" she said.

"We can try and redo it," said her mother, straightening her hat.

Her father looked at his watch. "Sorry, honey, I've got to go."

"But it looks awful," said Missy. "I can't show this to the class. Everyone will laugh at me."

Missy's father gave her a kiss on the cheek. "We'll do it again tomorrow morning before my performance. I promise."

"But, Dad . . ."

Mr. Fremont grabbed his viola case and headed out the door. "Don't worry. We'll fix it," he called. "I'll make it my number one priority. Even before the lawn."

Missy's arms dropped to her side. It didn't take a genius to see that things were not working out.

# CHAPTER

# 8

---

**M**issy wasn't even out of bed the next morning when she heard the phone ring. "It's for you," her mother called.

Missy ran to her parents' room and picked up the phone. "Hello?"

The person on the other end sneezed.

"Ashley?" said Missy.

"I need the camera back," Ashley said. "I forgot something. Is it okay if my dad picks it up in a few minutes?"

"But I'm not done with it," said Missy.

"I'll bring it back this afternoon," Ashley told her, "when I go to Stephanie's to shoot the finale."

"But I need it this morning," Missy said. "My dad has a matinee this afternoon."

"Sorry," said Ashley. She hung up before Missy could say anything else.

Missy sat quietly for a moment. Now what? The more she thought about it, the angrier she got.

It was all Stephanie's fault. If Ms. Perfect hadn't stolen her tape, she wouldn't be in this mess.

Missy stared unhappily out the window. Already people were coming and going at Stephanie's house. A musical equipment company unloaded an electric piano and drum set. A catering company brought plates of cold cuts wrapped in plastic. A large van with ZINK PRODUCTIONS written on the side carried in a truckload of stage lights and microphones.

Yuck, thought Missy. More than anything, she wished there were a way she could get inside Stephanie's house and look for her tape. Maybe if she and Baby were to wander over, no one would notice them.

Missy swung her feet to the floor. "Baby, where are you?" she called. "How would you like to go for a little walk?"

Ten minutes later Missy and Baby slipped out the front door. They carefully crossed the street and walked slowly past Stephanie's house. The front door was wide open and Missy could see Stephanie's father running around inside with some camera lights. Stephanie and Denise were nowhere to be seen.

"Follow me," Missy whispered. She and Baby darted across the Cooks' front lawn and made their way to the back of the house. Inside the Cooks' large family room Missy could see Stephanie's stage being set up. Several people were hammering away on the floor while another guy was moving large sheets of white cardboard around. Missy wandered through the sliding glass doors as if she knew what she was doing.

"Hey, pup," one of the guys hammering the stage said to Baby. The man held out his hand for Baby to sniff.

Missy gave the man a casual smile and then frantically scanned the TV cabinet with her eyes. She saw a stack of videotapes sitting on top of the VCR. "Baby, sit," she said. Her heart was racing ninety miles an hour. Calmly, she walked over to the VCR and carefully checked each tape. Hers wasn't there.

"What are you doing in here?" demanded a voice behind her.

Missy froze. "Hi, Stephanie," she said, turning around. "Our TV broke. I thought maybe I could catch *Lace Curtains*. Darryl just left Justine."

"You're kidding!" said Stephanie. She had her hair up in electric curlers. Her eyes suddenly narrowed. "Hey, wait a minute. *Lace Curtains* isn't on today. This is private property. You're trespassing."

Missy walked back over to Baby. "Okay, okay," she said. She looked around the room one last time.

"Out," said Stephanie, pointing to the door.

"All right," grumbled Missy. "We're going." She and Baby walked slowly back across the street. "Now what do we do?" she said as she let them both in the front door.

Missy heard the phone ring. "I'll get it," she called out.

It was Ashley and she sounded upset. "You'll

never believe what happened," she wailed. "I was coming down the stairs with the camera and my right ankle, the weak one, twisted. I fell down the stairs and the camera hit my foot and then smashed to the floor." She groaned. "I think my big toe is broken. It's all puffed up and my toenail is turning purple. I probably need crutches."

"What about the camera?" said Missy.

"It's not working," said Ashley. "My dad's going to have to take it to be fixed."

Missy couldn't believe it. Now she'd never have a chance to redo her tape. She could hear Ashley's mother telling her something in the background.

"I have to go to the doctor's now," Ashley said. She sighed loudly. "Stephanie's going to kill me. I can't be in her video now."

Missy stopped. "What did you say?"

"Stephanie's finale is going to be ruined," Ashley said. "She had the exact number of girls for each side of the stage. I was go-go position number three."

Missy suddenly had a brilliant idea. In her nicest tone of voice she said, "Why don't *I* take your place, Ashley?"

There was silence on the other end of the line. "But I thought you didn't like Stephanie," Ashley said finally.

"Whatever gave you that idea?" Missy answered sweetly. Her mind was racing. If she could just get back inside Stephanie's house, she could look for her tape again! She was sure it was there.

"What about a costume?" Ashley said.

"I can wear yours," Missy replied. "We're about the same size, aren't we? You can drop it off on your way to the doctor's."

"Are you sure Stephanie won't mind?" said Ashley.

"Of course not," Missy answered. "She'll be glad you found a replacement on such late notice."

Ashley sniffed loudly. "I guess you're right." With a loud groan she said, "I hope they don't put a cast on my foot. I hear they itch." She paused. "Sorry about the camera."

"That's okay," Missy said grandly. "I won't be needing it anymore. I hope you feel better." She hung up the phone and let out a loud whoop. "Watch out, Stephanie Cook," she said. "Go-go position number three is on the warpath."

Several hours later Missy was standing in front of her mother's full-length mirror checking herself out. "I look terrible in this thing," she said, tugging on Ashley's costume. "The top is too big and the bottom is too little."

Baby, who had been watching her, barked in agreement.

Missy sighed and then put her coat on. "Too late now," she said. "Ashley told me I was to be there at two sharp."

Baby followed Missy across the street. She looked at her watch. Right on time.

Stephanie answered the door still wearing her electric rollers and about five pounds of makeup.

When she saw Missy she gasped. "What are *you* doing here?"

"I'm taking Ashley's place," Missy said calmly. "She twisted her ankle and can't do it." Missy opened her coat so Stephanie could see her costume.

Stephanie held out her arm and blocked the door. "Oh, no, you don't," she said. "I won't let you ruin my movie."

"But you won't have an even number of girls," said Missy innocently. "It'll be more ruined if you don't let me fill in. I'm go-go position number three."

Stephanie paused.

"Ten minutes to shooting," Stephanie's father called.

"Oh, okay," she snapped. "But you'd better not wreck anything." She pointed to a door. "The other girls are in the family room. And leave your dog outside."

"Okay," Missy nodded, heading in that direction. As soon as she saw Stephanie disappear around the corner, she took a deep breath and raced upstairs.

The door to Stephanie's room was open. Missy darted inside and began frantically searching for the tape. It wasn't on Stephanie's desk or under her bed.

From downstairs someone called, "Five minutes to places."

Missy glanced around the room. On top of a long bookshelf she could see something that looked like a tape. She pulled Stephanie's desk chair over and reached onto the shelf. "Darn," she said. It was only a cardboard box with some hair ribbons inside.

"Places, everyone," shouted someone downstairs.

Missy quickly climbed off the chair and hurried back to the family room.

"Missy!" said her friend Emily. "What are you doing here?"

"Ashley twisted her ankle," Missy said. She was feeling so discouraged. She needed more time to look.

Stephanie's mother led all the girls to their spots along the stage. Stephanie was supposed to emerge from a cloud of mist at the back of the stage singing "I'm a Rock and Roll Girl."

Missy tugged on the bottom of her costume unhappily. This wasn't the way it was supposed to work out. What was she doing here in this stupid costume anyway?

"Action," yelled Mr. Cook.

From the back of the stage a hissing sound released the mist. Several girls coughed. Above the stage a silver mirrored ball began to spin.

Stephanie stepped out of the mist and the music started. She was wearing pink spandex tights and a fancier version of Missy's costume.

"I'm a rock and roll baby," Stephanie crooned, "a rock and roll girl . . ." She threw her arm out and accidentally hit the mirrored ball. "Ow!" She sucked on the end of her finger. "My nail broke."

"Keep going, Steffie honey," said her father. "Camera's still rolling."

Stephanie quickly managed to catch up.

Now the other girls lining the stage began swaying back and forth and clapping. "Ooo-ee, ba-by, ba-by," they sang. Missy reluctantly joined in.

Stephanie shook her rear end and spun around. All the other girls did the same—except Missy, who accidentally turned the wrong way. That's when she heard her costume start to rip.

Cautiously, she moved a tiny inch to the right. *R-r-ip* went the back. It was time to do another spin. Missy held her breath and turned as carefully as she could. This time the noise was even louder. *Rrr-i-p.* Stephanie gave her a dirty look.

Missy gestured sheepishly. "Costume's ripping," she said. She slid her hand over her rear end. The rip was about three inches long and growing. Good thing she was wearing tights.

She heard Emily calling her name. "What?" she said, covering the rip with her hand. She noticed everyone looking at her.

"It's your turn," whispered Emily. "You're supposed to point to Stephanie and sing 'Love ya, Baby.'"

"By myself?" she said weakly. "No one told me I had to sing by myself."

"Now!" said Emily.

"Love ya, *Baby*," Missy sang, right on cue. The back of her costume burst open. Missy delicately backed her rear end up against the stage, hoping no one would notice. To her relief, Stephanie sang on.

Then from outside the family room Missy heard a familiar howl.

Missy tried to get Baby's attention to make him stop, but Baby's howls only got louder. Now Stephanie was looking around the room, trying to figure out what it was. As she hit a high note, Baby let loose. "*Aaooow, aaoow,*" he sang.

Emily and Amy started to giggle.

Stephanie finally noticed Baby. When she saw who was making the noise, she tried to sing louder. "Give me all your lovin'," she screeched at the top of her lungs. But the louder she sang, the louder Baby sang. Finally, Stephanie threw her hands over her ears. "Cut! Cut!" she shouted. She stomped over to where Missy was standing. "You're trying to ruin me, aren't you?" she said.

"No, I'm not. Honest. Baby just likes your voice."

Everyone except Stephanie laughed. "I knew I shouldn't have let you inside. Maybe you should leave."

Missy thought fast. She *had* to find that tape. "Can't," she said, pointing down. "Costume's ripped."

Everyone in the room tittered. Stephanie frowned and then hopped off the stage. "I don't care if there's a gap in the chorus line or not," she said, handing Missy her coat. "An empty space would be better than you. You can't even dance or carry a tune."

Missy's cheeks burned. What nerve! "Oh, yeah?" she said. "Well I'm not leaving until you give me back my tape!"

"What tape?" said Stephanie.

Missy folded her arms. Too late to turn back now. "The one you stole," she blurted.

Stephanie's eyes grew wide. "I did not!" she said.

Missy glanced around the room. Everyone was looking at her as if she was nuts. With a loud sigh, she grabbed her coat, wrapped it around her waist, and let herself out the family room door. "I know you have it somewhere, Stephanie," she called over her shoulder.

"You're crazy," Stephanie called after her.

Missy angrily grabbed Baby's collar and led him out of the yard. She had never felt so discouraged in her life. She was going to be the laughingstock of the whole school when she showed her tape on Monday.

# CHAPTER

# 9

On Monday morning Missy awoke to see her mother sitting on the end of her bed. "Time to get up," she said gently.

Missy groaned aloud and pulled a pillow over her head. "Do I have to?" She thought about faking a stomach ache but she knew her mother wouldn't buy it.

"When do you show your tape?" Mrs. Fremont asked.

Missy dropped the pillow to the floor and dragged herself out of bed. "Two o'clock." She gave her mother a desperate look. "Maybe something will happen and Ms. Van Sickel won't get to mine. Maybe a tornado will come, or an earthquake."

"Don't count on it," said her mother.

"You're right," Missy said with a sigh. She walked over to her closet with a determined

expression on her face. "Oh, well. Might as well get this over with."

All day, Missy kept to herself. "How come you're so quiet?" Willie asked her during lunch. She'd already shown her videotape so she had nothing to worry about.

"I don't know," said Missy. "I guess I have a lot on my mind."

When the two o'clock bell rang, Missy's heart started to pound. Ms. Van Sickel smiled at the class.

"Okay, everybody, put away your books and let's have some fun." She walked over to the bulletin board. "Today we're watching tapes by Ashley, Stephanie, and Missy." Missy glanced at Stephanie, who stared back at her with a smug expression.

Ms. Van Sickel set the TV up and got one of the boys to lower the shades. "Ashley, let's watch yours first."

Ashley hobbled to the front of the room and put her tape into the VCR. On her right foot she was wearing an enormous fuzzy bunny slipper.

Ashley's tape opened with her giving a tour of her house. When she got to the kitchen, she showed everyone her pill collection. "This is a vitamin pill," Ashley said, "this one's for allergies, this is a calcium tablet . . ."

Missy yawned.

Next Ashley's mother told a family story about an uncle who had all his teeth pulled out so he could get dentures. Then after he got them, he discovered they made him choke. He had to spend the rest of his life without any teeth. "And do you know what the worst part was?" said Ashley's mother. "He was a dentist!"

Everybody got a big laugh out of that.

At the end of Ashley's tape she showed the class a safe that they had just discovered in their house. It was hidden behind a mirror on the stairway. Just as Ashley got to the safe and was about to open it, the camera crashed to the floor. Ashley flipped on the lights. "That's all," she said.

The class groaned. "Don't we get to see the safe?" said Adam Ramirez.

Ashley lifted her foot. "That's when I sprained my big toe and the camera broke." She looked over at Ms. Van Sickel. "Don't worry, my dad is having it fixed."

"What a rip-off," said David Holt. "The safe was the best part!"

Ashley gave him a dirty look and hopped back to her chair.

"Maybe Ashley can take a picture of her safe and bring it to class another time," Ms. Van Sickel suggested.

Ashley nodded.

Ms. Van Sickel walked to the front of the room. "Thank you for sharing that tape with us, Ashley," she said. "We enjoyed it, class, didn't we?" There was some polite applause.

Now it was Stephanie's turn. The knot in Missy's stomach felt as big as a basketball.

Stephanie tossed back her hair and flounced to the front of the room. She fiddled around with the volume. "Quiet, please. I can't hear." Finally she was ready.

A card flashed across the screen. *The Stephanie Cook Story*, it said. The videotape opened to a shot of Stephanie, sitting in a baby carriage. She was dressed in a floppy white baby's bonnet and sucking on a giant pacifier. "Hewo," she said in baby talk. She waved a stuffed animal at the camera. "I'm Steffie Cook and this is my story."

Missy squirmed uncomfortably in her seat.

"I was born in Methodist Hospital on April sixteenth at seven-thirty in the morning—an Aries with Libra rising. My mommy and daddy said I was adorable." She hugged the stuffed animal to show just how adorable that was. "When I was three years old, I started dance lessons at the Jordan School of Music. Here's what we did for our first dance recital when I was five."

The videotape switched scenes. Missy recognized several of the first graders, dressed in tutus. The cutest one was wearing a large sign around her neck that said "STEPHANIE—five years old." Naturally she was also the best dancer.

Missy glanced around the room. She saw Adam pretend to gag and Willie cover her mouth to keep from laughing. Maybe Stephanie's tape wasn't going to be so great after all.

The next scene was in Stephanie's bedroom. She sat down on her bed and pulled out an enormous scrapbook. "Here's me when I was born," she said, turning to the first page.

"You're not going to show us that whole thing, are you?" said David.

"Don't interrupt," Stephanie shouted at him. "People can't hear." She returned her gaze to the screen.

On camera, Stephanie was going through the scrapbook page by page. "Here's my third birthday party," she said. "We had a clown and pony rides."

Missy looked at the clock. The class was beginning to get restless. Finally Stephanie finished with her scrapbook. "And now," she said, "presenting the Stephanie Cook we all know and love!"

The scene switched to Stephanie's grand finale. Missy strained her eyes. There was so much mist that you could hardly see Stephanie, even with all her makeup on. Stephanie danced across the stage, singing slightly off-key.

Missy looked around the room to see if anyone else noticed. Emily and Amy were laughing.

"It's not supposed to be funny, you guys!" Stephanie snapped.

Now a couple of the boys started laughing too.

"Quiet down, class," said Ms. Van Sickel.

On screen, Stephanie was hopping around with a mike in her hand. She *did* look pretty silly, Missy admitted. Still, wait until people saw *her* tape. If they were laughing at this one, they'd *really* laugh at hers.

Missy heard some commotion in the back of the room. When she turned around she had the

shock of her life. "Grandma!" she exclaimed. "What are *you* doing here?"

Grandma had managed to squeeze herself into one of the empty desks. "Don't mind me," she was telling Adam Ramirez. "I'm just visiting my granddaughter, Missy Fremont." She saw Missy staring at her and waved. "Hi, lambkins."

Missy slipped to the back of the room. "How did you get here?" she whispered, giving Grandma a hug.

"In Alice," her grandmother whispered back. "How do you think?" She wiped her forehead with a tissue. "Never drove so fast in my life, either. But I knew how important it was to make it here on time. Did you show your tape yet?"

Missy looked puzzled. "No."

Grandma reached into her enormous handbag. "Good," she said, pulling Missy's tape out.

Missy nearly keeled over.

"I hope you'll forgive me," said Grandma. "I found it this morning under one of my scarves. I must've packed it by mistake. When I realized what it was, I called your mom. She told me you were showing it this afternoon at two." She fanned herself with a math book. "Can't believe I actually made it."

"What's going on in the back of the room?" said Ms. Van Sickel. She motioned to Stephanie to stop her tape.

"It's my grandmother," Missy said. "She's visiting me."

The whole class turned around. Ms. Van Sickel strained her eyes. "We have a visitor?"

"Verna Fremont," waved her grandmother. "Sorry to interrupt. Just pretend I'm not here."

"Oh," said Ms. Van Sickel. "Okay." She seemed slightly confused. "Please continue, Stephanie."

When Stephanie's videotape finished, the lights in the classroom came on and there was some scattered applause. "Very nice, Stephanie," said Ms. Van Sickel. "I would like to have seen a little more about the rest of your family. Does anyone else agree with me?"

Almost every hand in the class went up. "Hmm. Interesting," said Ms. Van Sickel. "Now, who's next?"

Missy waved her tape in the air. "I am!" She turned to her grandmother. "Can you stay?"

"Wouldn't miss it for the world." Her eyes twinkled.

Missy grinned and ran to the front of the room. She put her tape into the machine. As the class watched, Missy sat anxiously. She was relieved when everyone laughed at Baby's singing, and when it came to the part where Grandma sang, Missy could hear her grandmother singing along with herself on the tape from the back of the room. "Stereo," Grandma said, when Adam started giggling.

As soon as the tape finished, the class burst into applause. Everyone, that is, except Stephanie.

"Missy! That was wonderful!" said Ms. Van Sickel. "Maybe your grandmother would come up to the front of the class and talk to us some more."

"Yeah!" said several people at once.

"I'd be happy to," said Grandma, "only I'm stuck behind this desk."

While Missy helped pull Grandma out from behind the too-small desk, the rest of the class talked about her tape.

"I like Missy's tape the best," said Amy.

"Why?" said Ms. Van Sickel.

"It had the most about her family," said Leland Howe. "We learned about her ancestors."

Stephanie stuck her nose in the air. "But it wasn't very theatrical."

"What do you mean?" said Ann Leiber. "Everyone in her whole family is talented!"

Amy raised her hand. "Is it true Missy's grandmother played Miss Hannigan in *Annie*?"

"Sure is," said Grandma, weaving her way to the front of the room.

"Do you know any movie stars?" asked Meredith.

"I was in a play once with Paul Newman," she said.

"Wow," said Meredith.

Grandma told stories until the bell rang. "Don't forget about the history quiz tomorrow, class," said Ms. Van Sickel as people hurried to get their things together.

Missy gathered her books. Several students ran over to her with more congratulations while others asked for her grandmother's autograph. Missy glanced over at Stephanie. "Excuse me," she said.

She walked over to Stephanie's desk. "What do you want?" said Stephanie.

"I'm sorry Baby tried to ruin your song."

Stephanie shrugged.

Missy stared at the floor. "And I'm sorry I

accused you of stealing my tape," she added. "Grandma had it."

Stephanie folded her arms. "Humph! Imagine *me* stealing your tape!" She checked to see if anyone was watching them and lowered her voice. "Do you think your grandmother could get me Paul Newman's autograph?"

Missy stared at her. "I don't think so," she said, trying not to laugh. "That's when they were in high school together."

"Oh," said Stephanie. She looked disappointed.

"Hey, Missy!" interrupted Willie. "Come on! Your grandmother's going to take us all out for ice cream."

"I need some nourishment before my trip home," said Grandma.

"You aren't staying?" said Missy.

"Heavens, no," said Grandma. "I've got a rehearsal tonight. We're blocking the 'Poor Jud Is Dead' scene." She peered at the girls. "How many customers do I have?"

"Me, me, me," shouted everyone.

Missy turned to Stephanie. "Want to come?"

Stephanie's face brightened. "May I?"

"Sure!" said Missy. "There's room in Alice for the whole class."

"Follow me, chickies," said Grandma. As she led the way to the parking lot, she started singing. "Oh, what a beautiful morning, oh, what a beautiful day."

Missy grabbed Grandma's hand and joined in. "I've got a beautiful feeling," she sang at the top of her lungs, "everything's going my way, hey, oh, what at beautiful day!"